AM

"Deranged. Twisted. Violent. A Masterwork of Pulp-Cult Literature... Firmly lives up to everything you've come to expect of Davies' work."

"Fun, fast paced and with just enough violence and gore to have you asking for more. The writer of Hobo with a shotgun enthralls with a story of loss, regret, revenge and freedom. Do yourself a favor and dive in."

"Man vs Bear takes the reader into the depths of the depravity of Davies imagination... Fear the mother's scorn! Os!-Mi!-Um! Forever."

MAN VS BEAR

JOHN DAVIES

Extra Pulpy Books
extrapulpybooks@gmail.com

ISBN: 978-1-0696020-0-8

PROLOGUE
THE BAND

As his fingers slid across the fretboard, Mitch thought to himself, *This is what it means to be a man.* Hard work, sacrifice, and finally watching it all pay off. He looked up from his guitar to the packed arena in front of him, an ocean of ecstatic metalheads, all witnessing his band for the very first time.

Now, to leave them with something unforgettable. He ripped into his final solo, clinging to his sweaty pick, as he sped up, going faster, cranking the intensity until, with a flick of his wrist, he threw his pick into the audience and began to finger tap.

The crowd went insane, and Mitch ended his solo with a massive dive-bomb on the whammy bar.

That's when Dave, the band's new frontman, strutted center stage. Once his vocals hit, nobody could look away–not even Mitch.

The people adored Dave–his aggressive presence, the way he whipped his long hair like an animal.

As the final chord struck, the crowd erupted in whistles and screams.

Mitch clutched his guitar, soaking it all in, and he eyed his bandmates–Paul, Jeff, and Rick. They had just opened for SteelHaven, the biggest name in metal, and they had absolutely nailed it. *How the hell did they even get here?*

Dave grabbed the mic and threw a sweaty arm over Mitch's shoulder. "Thank you, Vancouver! I'm Psycho Dave, and these are my Flying Monkeys. You've been unreal... Now get ready for SteelHaven!"

Mitch's eyes widened in shock. "Wait, no!?" he said. "That's not our name!"

He saw his bandmates' mortified expressions as the audience chanted, "Psy-cho Dave! Psy-cho Dave!" But Dave just smirked as he waved to the crowd. Then he walked offstage without a word.

The back halls were a blur in Mitch's head, and the feeling in his gut was making him sick. He couldn't quite make sense of it all.

Production assistants, roadies–everyone who passed them–shouted, "Psycho Dave!"

Once the band reached an empty hall, Rick, their keyboardist, blocked Dave's path and said angrily, "What is wrong with you? Psycho Dave and the Flying Monkeys? Our name is Osmium!"

The sound of hollering interrupted. "Where are they?" someone shouted.

Dave smiled at his band. "Don't embarrass yourselves." Then he turned to the legends of metal themselves as they came walking toward them.

"SteelHaven..." Jeff gasped.

Mitch watched in awe as Chris Rolanti, SteelHaven's lead singer, grabbed Dave by the shoulder. "Great stuff. That set was incredible, but I thought your name was Osmium."

"It is!" Rick told him.

"It was," Dave corrected. "It's a last-minute change."

Chris mulled it over. "...SteelHaven, featuring Psycho Dave and the Flying Monkeys." He smiled. "Now that sounds like a show people want to see! Think you can pull that off every night?"

"Hell yeah," Dave said.

"Awesome–hey, Billy." Chris turned to his entourage. "Tell the old openers they're out. We're taking Psycho Dave instead."

Jimmy Riffs, SteelHaven's lead guitarist, turned to Mitch and winked. "Killer riffs, man. Welcome to the scene."

Wow, Mitch thought, his eyes lighting up as he watched SteelHaven walk away.

Moments later, Dave entered their green room. "Well... we're on the tour," he said triumphantly. Then, he grabbed a beer from the fridge. "Probably time to celebrate."

The rest of the band entered behind him, and when they were all inside, Jeff closed the door.

Rick's voice cracked with fury. "You're a slimy son of a bitch! Do you get that? We hired you. You can't change *our* name."

"Chris Rolanti liked it," Dave answered.

"I don't care," Rick yelled. "Our name is Osmium–we're staying Osmium."

"Well, Osmium didn't land the tour–Psycho Dave did. And now you all have the pleasure of playing for me... in my band. Oh, and we'll be getting costumes."

"You're really pissing me off," Rick replied.

"Hey, man... Like you said, you guys wanted me. And look what happened–less than two months in, and it's been nothing but up. I think I've earned my say."

Rick shook his head. "You can't go behind our backs."

Dave picked up a bottle of whiskey and slowly poured each of them a shot. "Look, you want to get bigger? You want the rock 'n' roll lifestyle? Well, it seems you need me to get it. So if that's the way it is, it's got to be Psycho Dave's way–and Psycho Dave's music."

"What does that even mean?" Jeff asked him.

"It means no pussy shit. We only play the stuff I want. We're going to be the toughest metal band on the planet. You got that?"

"What about Osmium?"

Dave slammed the whiskey bottle down and glared at them. "Osmium's dead."

A troubling silence filled the room. The band exchanged concerned looks of dread. Dave was taking over.

Rick responded defiantly, "And if we say no?"

"Then I get a new band... and you get a new singer. But I'll warn you–it's me they love."

Jeff laughed nervously. "This is a joke, right?"

The silence stretched.

"Make up your minds..."

After a long pause, Paul turned to Mitch. "Mitch, you haven't said much. What do you think?"

They all looked at Mitch and waited.

He didn't like it. He felt betrayed. Osmium was something they had built together; a piece of each of them was part of it. But after years of mediocre gigs, financial struggles, and protecting it all from ruin, Dave's vocals *had* elevated them to where they were today. Maybe it wouldn't be so bad to trust his vision.

"What we did out there," Mitch said, pointing toward the stage, "was legendary. The people were going wild for us. It's honestly everything I've ever wanted. I can't let this slip away."

Rick shook his head. "We're going to lose ourselves, man."

"I don't know, dude," Jeff interjected. "The way it felt behind that kit, with all those people going crazy like that…I want to do it again. I'm with Mitch."

Paul's eyes moved back and forth, between Rick and Mitch, weighing their opinions, then he decided. "Mitch, if you're cool with it, then I'm in too."

Rick picked up the first shot. "I guess that's it then. Osmium's dead. Long live Psycho Dave and the Flying fucking Monkeys."

Dave patted Mitch on the back. "Thanks, buddy." Then they all raised their shots as Dave toasted, "To the Flying Monkeys. I wouldn't be here without you." He gave them an ironic wink as they clinked glasses and sealed the deal by downing their whiskey.

1

THE GETAWAY

Trees towered overhead, and asphalt crumbled beneath the tires of Mitch's worn-out truck as it rumbled through an old northern forest.

His acoustic guitar, the one his father gave him, was in the backseat, next to his backpack, and the Grateful Dead's *Friend of the Devil* poured from the speakers.

He tapped the steering wheel as he drove, drumming to the song's melody. He wanted to be like Garcia–unburdened and free–just him and the strings.

"*This shit is soft, Mitch!*" Dave's words snapped in his head, making him wince.

He quickly jabbed the stereo, turning it to Mötley Crüe, and cranked the volume. This was the kind of sleaze and swagger the band wanted from him.

He thrust his hand out the window and belted the chorus, "*Girls, Girls, Girls*."

Buzz. His phone vibrated, and he glanced to see who was calling. His face soured.

"*I can't answer you,*" he said with frustration.

Eventually, the buzzing stopped, and a notification popped up on the screen: 'O*ne missed call, one new voice message.*'

He ignored it and drove on.

Soon, a gas station came into view, tucked within the trees along the road. Mitch pulled in, parking next to the only pump as he killed his engine and stepped outside.

The crisp spring air filled his lungs, rejuvenating him while he stretched. "This is what I need," he said. "Some good old-fashioned Mother Nature."

He put the nozzle in his gas tank and watched as the numbers ticked up.

Moments later, a bell jingled as Mitch entered the station.

Country music played softly against the low hum of refrigerators, and nobody was at the register–no customers either–the place looked abandoned.

The beer must be in the back, he thought, and he headed deeper to have a look.

The shelves were filled with trinkets, mini totem poles, hunting supplies, snacks, and even bear mace.

A woman's voice hummed gently in the next aisle, and then he saw her, stocking the fridge with beer cans from a basket on the floor.

"Got any cold ones?" he asked.

She jumped up. "Oh my goodness, I didn't hear you come in."

She looked at him, and her beauty was undeniable–blonde curls, a face fit for an album cover, and a body that should have stirred something primal inside of him–but it didn't.

"Sorry, I scared you," he said, brushing past her to the fridge.

"It's okay."

He grabbed a case of beer, and then his eyes scanned the shelves. "Where's the Jack?"

"It's locked under the counter," she told him. "I'll get you some."

She led the way, talking as he followed. "I can't believe I didn't hear the doorbell. You ever just get lost in your thoughts like that?"

Constantly, he thought, and then he watched her go behind the counter and unlock the cabinet underneath. "What size?" she asked.

Dave's advice ran through his head, *"Get trashed...write thrash*. It's all that matters"

"The biggest one you got," Mitch answered.

She slid the bottle into a paper bag. Then, as she turned to Mitch, her eyes widened, and she realized who he was. She gasped, "Wait a second... No way. Are you one of the Flying Monkeys?"

Mitch cringed. He hated it when people called him that. "How did you know?"

Her face lit up. "How could I not know? I heard your new song on the radio, and I love it. I watched all your videos and interviews. Is the rest of the band with you? Is Dave here?"

Mitch scoffed. "No, it's just me."

"Oh man, what's he like?" she asked, twirling her hair. "He looks so intense."

The last year of Dave's psychological abuse flashed through his head: the rules, humiliations, threats, betrayals.

"He is intense," he told her.

She beamed. "That's hot," then she slid the bag toward him, making sure her fingers grazed his. "You're hot too… I'm surprised you're not *buried* in groupies right now." She leaned forward, revealing her cleavage. "*I* could be your groupie."

He gave the girl a fake smile. "I'm gonna be busy. I need to write some music." Then he pulled out his wallet and handed her a couple of bills. "Keep the change."

He started to walk away.

"Wait!" she called out. "My girlfriends are huge fans too. Maybe… a few of us could meet up? Have some fun?"

She bit her lip. "It could inspire you."

Mitch stopped and paused. *What the hell was a girl like this even doing out here?*

"What're their names?" he asked with a sigh.

Her lips curled mischievously. "Lena, Katie, and Jane."

"And you?"

She pointed to her name tag. “I’m Laura,” she said with a grin.

The name twisted something deep, and Mitch turned abruptly toward the door. “I gotta go.”

“What did I say?” she cried as he headed for the exit. “Can I at least have your autograph?”

The bell jingled as Mitch left, stomping to his truck. He yanked open the door, jumped inside, and muttered, “I need a fucking drink.”

2

LAURA

The sun set, and the night grew dark as Mitch clenched the steering wheel with one hand and finished his beer with the other.

He cursed the name of the girl at the station. *Laura–why did her parents name her that? Didn't they know how a reckless, no-strings night with their slut of a daughter and her friends might've just broken his funk and saved his career?*

He shook his head in frustration, "Why can't I forget about you?" Then he gulped down the last of his beer and chucked the bottle out the window.

"This shit's too weak," he snarled, and the glass shattered against the road.

Mitch's hand reached into the paper bag, and he pulled out the whiskey. If he was going to write the kind of music Dave wanted, he needed to embrace the destructive nature that went with it.

He propped a knee against the wheel and twisted off the cap before taking a long swig–it burned going down and made him feel reckless.

His foot pressed hard against the gas, and the trees blurred past him as the truck began to swerve. He cut back and forth between the lanes, chanting, "Os-mi-um! Os-mi-um!"

Then he took another swig, and the bottle sloshed, spilling over his chin. He laughed–unhinged–until he felt a soft hand calming him. It was an unmistakable touch, and for a second, he sank comfortably into the memory.

"Laura..." he mumbled, remembering his ex. He felt her lips brush his neck.

Then the fear of Dave's wrath cut into him like a knife to the back. "No!"

He pressed the whiskey to his lips and started to chug, chasing away her memories. But even after she'd gone, her kiss still lingered and aroused something inside of him.

He diverted his mind to the other Laura–the hot and desperate super-fan he'd met at the gas station. *Why didn't I just fuck her?* he thought angrily. He *was* single, wasn't he? That was the whole point.

He began to imagine her hot body and low-cut V-neck pressed over the counter as he squeezed his hands into her hips.

He shifted in his seat. It was becoming impossible to focus on the road.

He couldn't take it any longer and yanked his zipper down, letting his hand fumble in a frantic rhythm.

Finally, for a moment, he felt good, and then her name echoed in his mind–*Laura*–twisting his fantasy, and summoning his ex. Her long black hair, the baby-pink lingerie that he loved–she wasn't angry. She smiled, kissed him.

He gripped harder, lost in her memory.

Pleasure surged, and he glanced up, catching a glimpse of his own insanity in the rearview mirror. “Fuck it,” he said madly, “this is the wild.”

And with no one around to judge him, Mitch let go across the steering wheel, and released the tension that was inside.

His eyes closed in a moment of relief, and when they opened, a small animal was in the middle of the road and right in front of his truck.

“Shit!” he blurted, swerving. But it was too late.

THUD! The creature smashed against the grille and rolled beneath him as he hit the brakes. The truck skidded hard, burning rubber across the road. Then it came to a sudden stop, hurling Mitch face-first into his own sticky mess.

3

MOTHER

Mitch groaned, lifting his head from the wheel. “What did I hit?” he asked, and he wiped the spunk off his face.

He fumbled for the door, cracking it open and stumbled outside with a drunken wobble.

Clouds filled the night above, covering the moon, and the cold breeze had picked up, making him shiver.

He tucked himself back into his pants as he made his way behind the truck and toward the animal he had just hit.

A faint whimper grew as he got further from the taillights, and with each step, the sick guilt he felt intensified.

And then he saw it—a small, mangled creature, crawling toward the forest.

"Oh no…" Mitch gasped, and he slowly moved closer, hoping to help. "Are you okay, little guy?"

He knelt down and awkwardly tried to reach out to touch its fur. But then, as the animal turned to him, he fell back, mortified.

It was a bear cub, with a snout cracked open, and teeth hanging from its broken jaw. Blood gushed down its little face as the poor, desperate creature started to wail.

"No, please be quiet," Mitch begged, trying to hush the animal. But there was no hope. Within seconds, he heard the pounding of heavy paws and saw the glow of the giant mother bear's eyes as she burst from the woods ahead of him.

Terrified, he turned, stepping through the cub's blood, and sprinting back to his truck.

She was gaining on him as he grabbed the door, and he jumped inside, just as—*BAM*!

A massive force struck his vehicle, engulfing it with fur and muscle, and Mitch watched in terror as the mother's claws scraped across his windshield.

He stomped the gas, but the tires went nowhere. "Why isn't this thing moving?!" he cried.

Then *SMASH!* The bear's head broke through his driver's side window, and he ducked as her spitting mouth and gnashing teeth pushed inside.

In his terror, he noticed he'd left the vehicle in park.

His hand shot out, shifting into drive and he hit the gas as she snarled.

The tires gripped, and the truck threw the mother bear off as it fishtailed away.

Mitch lifted his head, steadying the vehicle, and he looked into his rearview mirror. The bear was running back to her lifeless cub as she faded into the night, and for minutes after, he could hear her mournful howls echoing through the forest.

4

HIDE AND SEEK

Mitch drove like he was fleeing a crime scene, knuckles squeezing the wheel, his eyes bugged open at the road. "What the hell is wrong with me?" he yelled.

The bear, the booze, his dick in his hand as it all happened. It ran through his head like a drunken loop of terror and self-loathing.

Suddenly, the GPS voice spoke up from his phone, "Your destination will be on the left, in one kilometer."

"No," he gasped. "That's too close." He looked over his shoulder, in the direction of the bear. "...Hey, Google, how far will a mother bear hunt someone down if they killed her cub?"

An AI voice responded, "An angry mother bear could chase someone for miles by following their scent."

He began to sweat. "Wait, seriously? What if I drove away?"

"Oh, if you drove away, then she'd stop once she couldn't see you. Bears don't hunt people or seek revenge."

"But you just said she would."

"I stand by what I said. A mother bear would likely not chase you down, especially if you drove away."

The GPS voice cut in, "You have reached your destination."

Confused, Mitch turned his truck into the driveway and illuminated the cabin with his blood-coated headlights.

He parked by the porch and hopped out, with his guitar, backpack, and booze.

When he reached the front door, a welcome mat lay waiting at his feet. It had an unsettling message printed in big bold letters, '*Welcome to Bear Country.*'

His nerves shook as he flipped it over and found the key hiding underneath. He entered the cabin and locked the door behind him.

It was dark inside, and Mitch leaned against the wall as he took a deep breath. "I can't believe it," he said, and he began to laugh nervously. "I survived a bear attack..."

He left the lights off as he walked into the living room and crashed down into a fur-skinned armchair. He dropped his booze, and bag beside himself and smiled.

"Man, I got to write a song about this."

He grabbed a beer, popped the top, and took a long swig. When he set it down, he grinned at the guitar in his hand. If Dave had it his way, this acoustic would have been destroyed long ago.

"Acoustic guitars are made for sad boys," he always said. *"So they can tell the world how sad they are."*

What did Dave know? This acoustic had been Mitch's personal act of defiance. Almost every song he'd ever written for the band, even their biggest ones, had been with it.

Mitch strummed the guitar, warming up the strings. It was time to save his spot in the Flying Monkeys.

He started playing a melody and making up words. *"Those haunting eyes and wailing cries,"* he sang softly. *"Why'd I leave you by the road?"* Then he stopped, and his body tensed as he squeezed the neck of his instrument.

"*No pussy shit,*" he hissed. He was going to write the hardest thrash metal Dave had ever heard, on this acoustic, just to spite him.

He picked up his bottle of beer again, took another long drink, wiped his lips, and declared, "*Get trashed, write thrash.*"

He started to play, faster, letting the alcohol control him, and he sang like Dave would–angry, demented, and above all, psychotic.

"*I killed her, she's dead, her mama's after me, killing me, killing me, killing me...*"

He stopped suddenly, grabbed his backpack and pulled out a pen with his notepad. "I got to write this shit down."

Then, as he started to jot down his lyrics and ideas, he heard a metallic noise creaking outside.

The music vanished from his head, and he rushed to the window. Slowly, peeling back the curtains and peeking outside.

Everything was silent and still. His truck sat near the cabin, and a cool wind blew through the trees. Then something moved, and he saw her sniffing around his truck and into view.

"No," he gasped, and shivers ran down his spine as she began rubbing her nose against his bloody grille.

Dear God! She followed the blood.

Mitch's eyes were glued to her as she grew more ferocious by the moment, and he watched as she rose on her hind legs and began rocking his truck, back and forth–harder and harder–until she flipped the whole thing over.

Then, the terror really struck him as she dropped on all fours and started sniffing her way toward the front door.

"Holy shit," he gasped, and he turned, running further into the cabin and looking for an escape or a place where he could hide.

CRACK!

Mitch ducked behind the kitchen island, and as he did, the front door and the frame around it splintered off the wall.

He froze still as she entered, and he listened to her breaths. She was following his footprints, and nervously, his eyes moved to the bottom of his boots. *Shit!* The cub's blood was caked in his treads.

I need to get out of here, his mind screamed.

Then, he heard the mauling of the living room furniture, his heart skipped a beat. Suddenly, the armchair he had just sat in came smashing against the dining room wall.

The bear's sniffing grew louder as she followed his scent directly toward his hiding spot. He couldn't stay here, and he started to creep silently, rounding the island to stay out of her vision, and as he did, he saw a door down the hallway. It was his only chance, and he dashed.

Mitch's boots scuffed the floor, alerting the bear as her head perked up, and like a missile, she leapt onto the island counter, dashing across before launching herself at him.

Mitch grabbed the handle of the door, twisting as he pushed it open.

SLASH! The tips of her claws tore across his back, and he fell into the next room, cut open and bleeding as he hit the floor. He rolled over and saw the bear, with her fierce maternal eyes and snarling jaw, stalking toward him.

He kicked, catching the door and slamming it shut. Then, as she roared and banged angrily on the other side, he jumped up and dashed for the ensuite bathroom.

Mitch made it inside, locking himself in, and looked frantically around as he asked, "*What do I do? What do I do?*"

The bedroom door broke down, and the sniffing grew until she was just outside the bathroom.

He could hear her breathing now, and needed a weapon, fast.

The medicine cabinet flew open; Nothing. Then, the shower; Nothing still.

The door started to shake as he ripped open the side drawers of the sink, and then finally, he looked in the cupboard beneath.

Cleaning supplies, tons of it.

SMASH!–The door exploded in as Mitch grabbed a bottle of concentrated bleach and twisted off the cap.

The walls creaked and bent as the bear pushed her bulk in through the frame, and Mitch started to shake the bottle, splashing the contents across her face and fur.

As the bleach hit her, she went mad, exploding in agony, and he could feel the pain within her as she wailed.

The bear pawed at her eyes and backed out of the room.

For a moment, Mitch stood motionless, listening to her tortured cries. Then, as he looked around the bathroom, he realized there was no way out but past her.

He stuck his head through the broken doorway and saw the bear, rubbing her face against the carpet and sobbing. Then, when she lifted her head, she began tearing at the bleach with her claws.

Blood, fur, and chunks of flesh flung across the room, and as Mitch looked on, she stood, swinging her head madly until suddenly she pointed her mangled face directly at him.

What had she done to herself?

Her eyes were gone, gouged out completely. All that remained were the oozing sockets, torn muscle, and bleeding veins.

She swung her head away in confusion.

She can't see me, he realized, and then he thought, *Go! Now!*

Mitch ran for the broken doorway, and the bear's head turned at the sound. She huffed, blowing blood and snot from her sinuses, and she charged.

Mitch made it out, just as she crashed into the wall beside him. Then he kept running–through the kitchen, the living room, and finally, he grabbed his acoustic guitar as he fled the cabin completely.

5

REGRET

Mitch passed his toppled truck as he ran, and he could hear the bear wailing inside the cabin behind him.

As the sound grew further, he wondered if she would die in there, and he pushed through the pain of his torn-open back as he ran.

What if I die? he thought. *What if I never make it out of these woods? What would my life have been? Mitch Jamison, guitarist for a band that didn't like his music, and guy that dumped the girl of his dreams.*

He thought of Laura, and how that song he had written for her had become such a success. It made him choke up.

"How could I have left you?" he asked desperately.

But he knew exactly why–*Dave–that fucking bastard*.

Those psychotic eyes burned in his mind as he ran, and he remembered the band surrounding him in the jam spot. His former friends who were nothing but Dave's mindless goons now.

"Your girl has to go," Dave told him.

"Why?" he'd asked.

Then Dave held up some hipster metal magazine. '*From Psycho to Sell-Out*,' the front cover read.

"Do you see this?" he seethed. "They're calling us sellouts because of your stupid love song."

"Every radio station is playing it," Mitch told him. "I mean, come on... It's made us the biggest thing out there."

Dave scowled, "We didn't start this band to churn out some lame radio garbage..."

Mitch looked back at Dave with utter rage. "You didn't start this band at all..."

The room went silent, and finally, Dave told Mitch spitefully, "She goes, or you go!" And then the band nodded along, agreeing with him.

Mitch was speechless, and he knew there was no arguing. He would either have to listen to Dave or leave the band he had helped create.

"Take out your phone," Dave told him. "Call your stupid girlfriend, and end it now. No sweet goodbyes, nothing, you dump her and never talk to her again."

Mitch felt sick with guilt over what happened next. He had called her and dumped her cold with Dave standing there, smiling. And then he hung up without giving her a single reason why.

"Aw, good work, buddy," Dave said. Then he opened his arms and embraced Mitch, pulling him close as he whispered into his ear, "Now, find the old fire–or you're out."

Suddenly, Mitch's throat burned, and he stopped on the road, lurching forward and vomiting up his alcohol.

The booze and bile hit the asphalt, splashing back onto his pants, and he stood there, keeled over.

Drool hung from his mouth as he stared into the puddle and listened to the utter silence around him. With no sign of the bear, he suddenly felt courageous, "Fuck you, Dave," he said. "I'm calling her."

He pulled his phone out from his pocket, scrolled to Laura's number, and paused as he felt the weight of his decision.

Dave always found out everything. If he made this call, his career would be over. Dave would kick him out for sure. But what did it even matter? The band was making him miserable.

He hit the button and listened nervously as it rang.

The ringing continued, and in the pauses between the tones, Mitch started to worry.

What if she doesn't want me back, and this was a mistake? I could lose everything.

He could feel more alcohol bubbling up in his throat. Then suddenly, *BLECH!* He tossed up a mouthful of bile.

"Yuck," he groaned, and as he did, he heard a shuffle and then the familiar sound of Laura's busted AC rattling in his ear.

" L-Laura?"

There was no response.

"Laura, I know you're angry with me, and you have every right to be, but you have to hear me out. I never wanted to break up with you. It was Dave..."

She cut him off, "Mitch..."

A giant smile crossed his face as he heard her voice. "Laura! It's so good to hear you. I miss you so much right now, you have no idea."

His eyes darted in the darkness as she answered, "Did you even listen to my messages?"

Shit. "Messages? No, I..."

She cut him off. "I should have figured... You're a selfish bastard, and you sound drunk. You have no idea the hell you put me through."

"I'm sorry, I..."

Click–the line went dead.

"Laura?"

He pulled the phone away from his ear and stared at the screen in confusion. He had to hear those messages.

Anxiously, he scrolled to find them, but before he could, he heard a sound rumbling down the road his way.

Is that the bear? No, it was heavy metal. Loud and thrashing. A vehicle approached, and as its headlights grew closer, Mitch slowly moved toward it, waving his hands and shouting, “Stop! I need help!”

The vehicle slowed to a halt, and the music became quiet. The driver’s side door opened, and a man stepped out, nothing more than a blur behind the blinding beams. He shouted, “Hey, you alright?”

“I need a ride to the hospital!” Mitch told him.

He could feel the blood running down his back and onto his legs.

The driver walked into the light and revealed himself to be a young man with long shaggy hair and wearing an Iron Maiden t-shirt. He walked toward Mitch as two more guys emerged from the vehicle and looked on to see what was happening.

One of them shouted, “Yo, you play guitar?” And he pointed at Mitch’s acoustic.

The other said, “That’s dope, do you know any Slayer?”

“Listen, we’re in danger,” Mitch pleaded to them, “I–I was attacked by a bear... She might still be out there following me...” Mitch looked behind him, scared she’d be right there.

“I don’t see no bear,” one of the passengers said.

Then another interrupted, “Yo... I recognize you! You’re the guitarist for Psycho Dave and the Flying Monkeys. You’re famous!”

“Holy shit,” the driver said, “You’re right.”

Then all three of them quickly surrounded Mitch, looking at him in awe, and studying his face like some kind of specimen.

Mitch stumbled backwards, beginning to feel weak as his blood ran down his boot and onto the road.

“Please, I’m bleeding,” he begged. “We have to go.”

The driver looked down and finally noticed the blood dripping from Mitch’s body. His smile dropped, and he turned to his friends, “Yo, throw the beer in the trunk. We need to get this guy to a hospital.”

“Whoa,” one of the friends stammered as they saw the blood, and then the third, who was drunker than Mitch, shouted, “Make room for the rockstar.”

The metalheads went back to the vehicle and started moving the cases, but the drunk one returned quickly with a beer and said, "Hey, you want a drink? Sure looks like you could use one."

Mitch shook his head and answered painfully, "No."

"Alright," he said, "suit yourself," and then he popped the cap off, claiming it as his own with a nice long sip. "Yo, by the way, Psycho Dave rules, obviously, but that love song? Weak, man. Stick to the heavy shit." He let out a shameless burp, "Oh, hey, can you hold my beer? I need to take a leak."

Mitch took the bottle and watched as the man ran off into the trees.

"Seats cleared," the driver said. "We can put your guitar in the back." Mitch turned to the vehicle and started walking towards it when he heard a blood-curdling scream from the woods.

The drunk guy came running, zipping up his urine-soaked pants and screaming, "MONSTER!!!"

And then, the mutilated beast burst from the woods, bounding with fury, and within seconds, she pounced, sinking her claws into the man's body, and they could all hear the *CRUNCH* as her teeth broke through his skull.

"DANNY!!!" the two remaining guys screamed in horror.

With warm blood dripping from her teeth, she lifted her pus-oozing face and leapt toward the screams.

Mitch dropped the beer and his guitar as he backed away and ran. The cries of utter agony echoed behind him, and then, when the screams became silent, he looked over his shoulder and was horrified to see that the bear wasn't just chasing him; she was catching up.

6

THE FALL

There was no way he could lose her on the open road. She was too fast, even blind, so he cut into the woods. Swerving through the trees and jumping over stones, he tried to weave a path too difficult for the bear to follow. But as he looked back, he saw her silhouette darkened against the vehicle's shining headlights, and as he kept running, he constantly heard the snaps and cracks of trees behind him as she followed.

The woods grew darker, and the canopy thickened overhead. Suddenly, he could barely see anything. Unseen roots tripped his feet, branches scratched across his face and body, and still, he could hear her follow.

Mitch continued, running blindly when the ground sloped, and soon, he found the momentum taking him.

The hill was getting steeper, and he was bounding now, too fast to stop without wiping out, and then he hit a rock, and the pain exploded through his foot as he fell.

Every bump bruised him as he tumbled down the slope, and he hit the bottom with a giant *THUD*.

Mitch lay there, still, as the clouds opened above. It began to rain.

"Ugh," he groaned, too sore to move. He felt like the universe wanted him dead, and who knows, maybe it did. Maybe he deserved it. And as he lay there, ready to give up on life, his pocket started to *buzz*.

"Laura?" He reached a bruised arm into his pants and painfully pulled out the phone.

It wasn't her. It was a warning, *'Low Battery.'*

"No!" he said urgently. "You can't die now. I still need to hear her messages!"

So with his back still on the ground and the rain beating down on top of him, he scrolled, found them, and pressed play.

There were three. "*First message.*"

Her voice appeared, raw and broken, and he listened as the rain beat down on top of him.

"*Mitch, what is happening? Two hours ago, you kissed me goodbye and said that you loved me. I mean, you wrote me that song, there's got to be some explanation. Please call me...*"

CLICK. The message ended, and he felt sick.

It was the one she'd left, while he was still in the jam spot with the band. Dave had told him if he answered her–then or ever–he would be out.

"I'm such an asshole," he muttered. Then the messages continued.

"*I don't know if you found out somehow, but you need to call me...NOW.*"

CLICK

Huh? What was she talking about? Found out about what? He checked the date, and the message was left over a week and a half ago. The sickness in his gut only grew worse.

"Next message." The one she left just hours ago, while he was driving to the cabin.

"Wow, I guess you really meant it when you said I wouldn't hear from you again. Unbelievable. I genuinely thought this was real. I mean, Mitch, we talked about things, real things... Like a family." She whispered, *"I let you finish inside of me... because I trusted you."* Then she paused, *"Maybe this will make you laugh, since I guess this was all just a joke to you... I'm pregnant..."*

Mitch's earth shattered and his jaw dropped as he repeated the word, "Pregnant?"

Her voicemail continued, *"You left me when I needed you... And I'm not doing this alone. Mitch, I..."*

Her voice broke as the phone went dark, and died in his hands.

"No, no, no, no, no... Fuck! I need to talk to her..."

He tried to power it on, but the screen stayed dark.

"I can't believe it," he said. "I'm going to be a father."

And then he started to move his aching body, lifting it from the mud. One of his ankles was twisted from the fall, but he could still stand on the other, so he did, and he started to hop. Nothing was going to stop him from getting back to Laura.

7

BEAR FIGHT

Mitch's muscles burned as he hopped through the trees, chasing down the love of his life. He needed to get back to her, and when he saw a stick lying in the pines, he snatched it up and used it to run faster.

Even though the rain was loud, her furious roars were louder still, and they echoed from the woods behind him.

There was no stopping, and as he continued, he found a path in the forest and followed it.

The sound of rushing water came from ahead, and soon he saw a rope bridge through the pouring rain.

He sped up, hobbling faster, and when he reached the bridge, he looked over the edge to see a fifty-foot drop.

Water rushed below. One wrong move, and he would be dead. He looked at the ropes holding the thing together–badly frayed. The deck boards looked ready to snap.

This isn't safe, he thought. But, in his moment of doubt, he heard her roar again, and she was getting closer–fast.

He tossed the branch aside and grabbed the ropes, feeling the bridge creak and shake as he hopped on. "Take it slow," he told himself.

The rain came down hard, soaking him, and the wind pushed, but he held tight, making it halfway across before it all started to shake.

He fell to his knees. "What the hell?" he said, and he turned to look back.

There she was, wobbling onto the bridge and shaking it uncontrollably.

It was too dangerous to stand, so he stayed low, crawling on his hands and knees. Then, he heard the ropes snap and felt the planks falling out from beneath him.

The bridge had come undone, and Mitch plummeted, along with the bear, toward the ravine below.

SPLASH! he submerged into the icy depths, feeling the frigid grip of the water. Down he went, touching the bottom, and there he felt stillness. The world above was blurred to nothing, and he was alone. Momentarily invisible. Everything was silent, except for three words Laura had said, and they were repeating, incessantly, in his head, "I needed you."

He pushed up and kicked the water hard, swimming toward the surface and breaking through for a giant breath of fresh rain-filled air.

The ravine carried him downstream as his head turned about. *Where is she?* he wondered, but he couldn't see her. He couldn't see anything through the rain. Nothing, until the lightning struck.

The sky lit with tendrils of electricity, and the ravine illuminated in a show of sprawling white light. In it, Mitch saw an island of stones rising from the water ahead, and he swam toward them, cutting desperately across the water's rushing force.

The lightning paused, and the world became dark as he kept on swimming, hoping to reach the island and escape the rushing stream.

His hand struck a rock, and the pain told him he'd made it. He reached further, grasping the slime-covered stones and wrestling himself up until he could collapse beneath the pouring sky.

He lay there, feeling the shivers overtake him. Then, the lightning struck again, and with it, he saw his blood seeping across the rocks and into the rushing water around him.

Then he heard the splashing. *It was her. It had to be. She could smell his blood.*

Mitch rolled onto his hands and knees and rose onto his one good leg.

The splashing approached, and he could hear her powerful sniffs following him. He grabbed a stone, and as she got closer, he drew his hand back, ready to strike.

The lightning lit the sky again, and he could see her now, swimming through the water and then crawling onto his tiny island.

There was no more running. Nowhere left to go. Now, for what seemed like the first time, he had to fight, and he had to do it now.

He swung.

CRACK!

The rock shattered her snout, and she wailed, swinging her paw blindly, and striking Mitch across the side. He fell, knocking his head against a stone, and rolled, unconscious, into the water.

8

DREAMS

A breeze swept in with the summer dawn, picking up the scent of the jasmine incense, which rested on the windowsill.

Mitch lay across the bed, eyes open, sheets tangled around his body, and a chill lingering on his skin. Laura rested next to him, naked, beautiful, and pressed close. Her baby bump nestled safely in his hand. He rubbed her tummy with a big, silly grin on his face and felt as close to peace as he ever had.

It kicked.

"Did you feel that?" she asked.

"Yes," he said, amazed.

This was their future–a dream of happiness, a child's laughter, a family. He didn't need anything but this.

He pressed his ear to her belly and listened as it rumbled softly inside. Then Laura gave him a smile and asked, "Why are you so wet?"

Mitch looked down and saw that he was soaked–confusion hit–and suddenly the belly's rumbling grew into a terrifying rush.

The windows smashed open, and a flood poured in, devouring everything and pulling Laura away from him.

"Mitch!" she yelled, reaching for his hand as her face became submerged. He grabbed her and held tight, but as he did, the bear's paws reached around him from behind, and her claws dug in, tearing him open as the water pulled Laura away.

9

NATURE

Water lapped at Mitch's face as he lay, unmoving, across the wet stones of the riverbank. Suddenly, his lips quivered, and he muttered, "Laura," before his eyes flickered open.

To Mitch's wonder, he saw a magnificent show of light shimmering across the stream.

"Am I dead?" he groaned. *Had he drowned, or had that bear killed him in the ravine?* But as his eyes moved upward, he realized he was still very much alive.

High above him, the mythic lights of the aurora borealis moved like two emerald dragons, interlocked in careless play. And then, just as quickly as it came, it began to fade away. Replaced by the soft glow of dawn, and the promise that his night was almost over.

He pulled himself up from the shallow water and crawled toward drier land. The rain had stopped, and the sun brought a pale glow with a slight warmth that washed across the forest valley.

He craved even the slightest of its rays on his cold wet skin and stripped off his soaked jacket, taking his shirt with it. As the sun hit him, he smiled like a madman.

Nature had devoured him whole, and shot him back through her icy womb–reborn–and baptized in the savageness of the wild. Now, as he moved through trees and moss, hearing the insects and the birds waking for the day, he felt part of it–like they were one.

A moment later, he heard the faint growl of a truck drifting in the distance. The hunters were beginning their day. The woods would soon be filled with them. It was time to go home.

The trees thinned, and he saw the road ahead–flat, man-made, the beautiful trail that would take him away from here.

“I made it,” he said.

Now to wait. Mitch stood on the road, feeling alive, and listening to the sound of the wild all around him.

It wasn’t long before he heard another truck, approaching fast. His heart pounded as he waited, and soon two small headlights appeared in the early dawn. The vehicle approached, and as it did, Mitch noticed his legs growing shaky and his head beginning to spin.

The vehicle stopped, and he faltered as two men jumped out.

“He’s going down,” one said, and they both rushed toward him, grabbing his body as he collapsed.

10

RECKONING

The slam of a door woke him, and he heard a voice saying, “Dalton, call emergency.”

His eyes opened, and he was in the back seat of a truck, lying down and covered by a thick wool blanket.

What happened? he wondered. He was exhausted and had forgotten everything. *How had he gotten here?*

A distant voice spoke. *Who was that?*

A bearded man in the passenger seat held the phone to his ear. “He passed out once we found him…" he said. "Looks like he's been through hell."

Dalton turned and saw Mitch awake. "He's up," he told the person on the other end.

The driver locked eyes with Mitch through the rearview mirror. "Looks like you had a hard night," he said, "we're gonna get you help, okay."

Then Dalton asked, "She wants to know, are you one of those guys that got mauled by a bear?"

Suddenly, in his exhaustion, it all came back–the crash, the chase, Laura, the baby, everything–and he felt a surge of urgency as he remembered that he had to call her.

Mitch rose, pushing his aching body up in his seat–surprising Dalton as his hand shot out.

"I need your phone," he rasped.

"He says he needs my phone," Dalton told the operator–then he nodded and said, "Okay, we'll bring him in."

The call ended, and Dalton handed the phone to Mitch. "Call whoever you need," he told him–then he turned to the driver, "Swing her around, Roy. She says the hospital's the other way."

Mitch dialed fast and listened as it started to ring...

There was an answer, and he heard her voice, "*Yo, it's Laura, if you got something to say, you better say it.*" It was her answering machine.

He paused before he spoke, "Laura... It's me. I listened to your messages, and I want to raise this baby with you... I love you. I'm sorry I ever left." He held the phone to his ear for a moment longer–shivering–then hung up, and he passed it back to Dalton.

"Congratulations," Dalton told him. "Boy or girl?"

"I don't know," Mitch answered.

He had done what he could; now he had to wait and see what life would give him.

Roy shouted in terror, "What, in God's name, is that?"

Mitch's eyes swung to the road and he saw the bear charging straight for them.

"No!" He screamed, "How did she find me?"

"What's wrong with her face?" Dalton yelled.

Roy slammed the brakes and cut the wheel, screeching the tires while Mitch held onto his seat.

"What are you doing?" Dalton shouted, "Go through her!"

"And kill us all?" Roy responded in a frenzy, "Look at the size of that thing. She's a grizzly!"

They felt a drag as they turned–and all eyes whipped back to see the mother holding the tailgate with her powerful claws.

"She's got us!" Mitch shouted, and then she reached inside the bed and pulled herself inside.

Roy swerved the truck–veering back and forth–and as he looked into his rearview, he saw the gore across her face up close.

He turned to Mitch with a look of disgust– "What the hell did you do to her?"

He didn't respond; he just shivered in terror. Then Roy cut the wheel, too hard, and they began to flip.

The world spun into chaos as they barrel-rolled off the embankment and down a short hill–crunching metal and shattering glass, until Mitch slammed forward–pain exploding in his ribs as the truck crumpled against a tree.

The sudden stillness was broken only by the tick of the cooling engine and the drip of blood falling on Mitch's face. He took a deep breath and opened his eyes to see Roy slumped forward in his seat, a shard of windshield lodged in his throat, and blood spurting from his neck.

Mitch gripped the jammed door and pushed. "Come on!" he rasped, pounding against it until it opened, and then, with his ankle still twisted, he crawled out onto the forest floor.

A groan cut through the sounds of the woods, and Mitch saw Dalton's body twenty feet away, face down, and thrown from the vehicle–his phone began to ring.

"Laura," Mitch gasped–it had to be.

He crawled toward Dalton as he heard him choking on his own blood. "Help...," Dalton gurgled.

As Mitch reached him, Dalton's voice was frail and pleading. But what could Mitch do? He wasn't a doctor–instead, he ignored the pleas and reached into Dalton's front pocket, pulling out his cell phone, and answering, "Laura?"

"Mitch..." she replied.

"Laura," he rasped. "I'm coming back to you."

Silence.

"Laura?"

He waited for an answer, but was met instead with the sound of her quiet sobs.

"Please talk to me," he said. "I made such a big mistake. I want to raise this baby with you. I love you, Laura."

Her cries grew raw, and fear seized him. "Laura? Please," he begged.

Her voice broke through, filled with grief. "Didn't you finish the messages?"

"What do you mean? My phone died before the end." Mitch felt a pressure building in his chest, like he was trapped beneath the water.

"Mitch, I called you from the clinic. I thought I'd never hear from you... I didn't know what else to do..." she cried. "It's over. It's gone... Why didn't you answer me?"

Her weeping deepened, and the phone slipped from Mitch's hand, landing on Dalton's dead body.

Laura's voice echoed faintly, thick with tears. "Mitch... Mitch, are you there?"

He wanted to answer, but he couldn't; he was staring face-to-face with the mother bear. She had found him, and she was ready to finish what she had started.

He stared into the carnage that he'd created, and it was hideous, but behind the horror, and the snarls, and the tears, he heard the sad cry of a mother who had lost everything. His fight was gone; she had earned her revenge.

"Come and get me," he said.

Laura cried Mitch's name again as the bear charged, five hundred pounds of wrath, barreling straight toward him.

She swung her claws–creating four deep slashes that filled with blood across his chest. Then, she snapped, lunging out with her teeth and sinking them deep into his arm.

His screams tore out through the morning forest, and Laura shouted desperately as the bear chewed into him.

"Mitch, what's happening?" she yelled.

He wailed as the bear lunged at his face, and then writhed in pain as she pulled her head back, tearing one eye out from its socket.

Mitch watched with half his vision as the bear squeezed his eyeball between her teeth and popped it like a milky grape.

"Mitch?" he heard Laura yell again, and then the bear slammed her foot down on the phone and silenced her for good.

She rose up on her hind legs–raising her paws for the final vicious blow, and as she did, Mitch's life flashed before his eyes, and he wished he'd just stayed Osmium.

Then suddenly a shot rang out through the woods, and a scarlet haze burst from the bear's shoulder.

The mother turned to where the shot had come–then *BANG*! Another rang out, and a final spray of gore exploded from her head–misting as she fell.

Her massive body crumpled next to Mitch, and he stared at her with his one remaining eye.

"Why?" he said. *Why hadn't it been him? She deserved her revenge*.

Footsteps pounded through the trees, and two men sprinted toward Mitch.

"Get out the first aid!" one of them yelled, and then he said to Mitch, "Dear Lord, are you alive?"

Mitch groaned and heard the words, "Get me the gauze and the alcohol."

No more alcohol, Mitch thought as blood gushed from his face, blinding him as he felt the bandages wrap around his wounds. Then someone was talking to the emergency operator, and it all went quiet.

EPILOGUE
LONG RECOVERY

A small TV was mounted in the ceiling corner, right in front of Mitch's bed, where he could see it. A reporter spoke as the news played, "Mitch Jamison, guitarist for locally based heavy metal act, Psycho Dave and the Flying Monkeys, has survived a vicious bear attack."

The door opened, and a nurse entered. "You've got visitors," she said. Mitch groaned as he peeled his eye away from the TV.

"Who?" he asked weakly.

She smiled, "It's your band!" and she didn't even wait for his response before letting them in through the door.

This was the first time Mitch had seen them since they made him break up with Laura.

Paul looked shaken as he observed Mitch's condition, and Jeff kept his gaze to the floor the whole time. Dave, though–he was like a hawk, staring Mitch straight into his one remaining eye.

"Man, that bear really got you, didn't it?" Dave said in his smug and condescending way. "I hope you weren't trying to play her one of your love songs."

Paul spoke up, "The nurse said you might be able to use your guitar again. Not like you used to, but that's good, right?"

Mitch looked at Paul without expression.

"But you know," Dave interrupted, "in the meantime, we have to replace you. Can't just stop now, but don't worry, we got a guy, and he's *really* good. Actually, one of the best out there. Super *tough* riffs–the *hardest*."

"Good," Mitch said, unfazed.

Dave looked stunned at his response.

Mitch's mind had been filled with thoughts of Laura and his lost child, before and after he regained consciousness, and for whatever reason, the band no longer concerned him.

"You going to be all right?" Paul asked.

"Yeah, I'll be great."

"Well, we gotta get going," Dave said, "Band stuff, you know. Hopefully we'll see you around sometime... Oh, and feel free to come check out a show when you're out of this dump. I think you'll love it. We're better than ever."

Jeff followed Dave silently, and then Paul gave Mitch a sad look at the door before saying, "Miss you, brother."

The band left, and the days dragged on. At one point, the nurses even dropped off Mitch's acoustic guitar, which had miraculously survived the night and been recovered.

Three months of slow rehabilitation went by before his next visitor came.

"You have a visitor," the nurse told him.

"Who is it?" he asked.

"A young lady named Laura."

Mitch perked up; *she was here*.

"Send her in," he said, and then he smiled as the nurse left to receive her.

The seconds dragged, but soon the door opened, and Laura reappeared into his life, more beautiful than he remembered, but reserved and wearing a maturity he'd never seen before.

She looked at him and covered her mouth as she saw the scars and the wounds of all he had been through. It was too much, and she looked away.

"Oh, Mitch."

"You should see the other guy," he said dryly.

"I heard the screaming," she stammered, "The sound of it still keeps me up at night… A lot of things keep me up at night… I thought you were dead."

"So did I."

She walked up to Mitch and sat in the visitor's chair beside him, still avoiding the injuries with her eyes, and she took his hand. "You were the love of my life, Mitch," she told him, "I was so happy with you." Then there was a long pause as Mitch waited for her to finish. "In a different life, I know we'd have our happy ending."

"But not this one?" he asked.

She wiped a tear, shaking her head and squeezing his hand.

"I can't," she answered, then she looked at him, "I hope you do well, Mitch. You deserve to be happy."

She stood up and walked to the door, giving him her final words, "I wish it could be different." Then she left his life forever as the door closed behind her.

Mitch lay on his back, staring at the ceiling. The band was gone, the bear was dead, and Laura was lost, along with their unborn child.

He pressed the red button resting beside him, and soon the nurse appeared. “Can I get you something?” she asked.

“Yes,” he responded, looking to the corner. “Could you pass me that guitar?”

She smiled as she gave him the instrument. “I was hoping you’d pick it up.”

Then, after she’d left, he painfully started to pluck a few notes, and to his own surprise, he felt like Garcia–unburdened and free–just him and the strings.